Roanoke

The Mystery of the Lost Colony

LEE MILLER

SCHOLASTIC NONFICTION
an imprint of
SCHOLASTIC

To the after-school "Panther Club"
for their help on this book. — LM

Map of the Secotan Country by John White. Today, the coastal area of
the Secotan's homeland is known as North Carolina's Outer Banks.

contents

Historical cast *(in order of appearance)*

PEMISAPAN ~ Secotan leader. Also known as Wingina. Was murdered by Lane's men.

RALPH LANE ~ Commander in charge of the fort on Roanoke Island. Massacred the Secotan at Dasamonquepeuc where Pemisapan was killed.

SIR WALTER RALEIGH ~ Knight, adventurer, poet, inventor, queen's favorite. Sent expeditions to Roanoke Island.

PHILIP AMADAS ~ Raleigh's captain. With Barlowe, he led the first Roanoke expedition.

ARTHUR BARLOWE ~ Raleigh's captain. Led the first Roanoke expedition.

SIMON FERNANDEZ ~ Ship's pilot (guide) from the Azores. Sabotaged John White's colony.

GRANGANIMEO ~ Pemisipan's brother.

MENATONON ~ Leader of the Chowanoc.

QUEEN ELIZABETH ~ Queen of England.

SIR RICHARD GRENVILLE ~ Raleigh's cousin. Led the second Roanoke expedition.

MANTEO ~ Secotan ambassador from Croatoan. May have been the last to have seen the Lost Colonists at Roanoke.

WANCHESE ~ Secotan ambassador, probable relative of Pemisapan. Later led survivors at Dasamonquepeuc.

THOMAS HARIOT ~ Expedition scientist.

JOHN WHITE ~ Expedition artist, became governor of the City of Raleigh. Father of Eleanor Dare, grandfather of Virginia Dare.

ELEANOR DARE ~ John White's daughter. Married to Ananias Dare. Mother of Virginia Dare.

ANANIAS DARE ~ Bricklayer. Married to Eleanor, John White's daughter. Father of Virginia Dare.

CAPTAIN SPICER ~ One of Watts's captains. Drowned off the shore of Hatorask Island.

VIRGINIA DARE ~ First English child born in the New World, at Roanoke Island. Daughter of Eleanor and Ananias Dare. Granddaughter of John White.

ROBERT DUDLEY, THE EARL OF LEICESTER ~ Nobleman. Queen Elizabeth's long-time favorite. A friend to Raleigh. Ruthless to his enemies.

SIR CHRISTOPHER HATTON ~ Lawyer and dancer who caught the queen's eye. Always jealous of Raleigh.

WILLIAM CECIL, LORD BURGHLEY ~ Queen's treasurer and oldest adviser. Operated a spy network and was one of the most powerful men in the kingdom.

SIR FRANCIS WALSINGHAM ~ Queen's secretary of state. Operated the biggest spy network in the world and was *the* most powerful man in the kingdom. Bitterly disliked Raleigh.

ROBERT DEVEREUX, THE EARL OF ESSEX ~ Walsingham's son-in-law. A nobleman, he formed a clique against Raleigh.

JOHN WATTS ~ English businessman. Spain called him England's most notorious pirate. Wore expensive jewelry and gold chains.

CAPTAIN COCKE ~ One of Watts's captains. Took John White back to Roanoke to search for the Lost Colonists.

CAPTAIN NEWPORT ~ One of Watts's captains. Arm was cut off in the Caribbean in a fight with the Spanish.

ELIZABETH THROCKMORTON ~ One of the queen's maids of honor. Secretly married Raleigh and was thrown into prison.

KING JAMES ~ Scottish king. Became king of England at Queen Elizabeth's death. Ordered Raleigh to be beheaded.

JOHN LAWSON ~ Surveyor who found a clue about the Lost Colonists.

CHAPTER 1

Roanoke

1586, Dasamonquepeuc, the Secotan country.
Dawn crept across the shallow bay and over the sandy beach
with the stillness of death, for death was coming. Pemisapan,
the Secotan leader, must have known this. Surely he expected
it. How could he not? For a year, English troops had been in his
country and death had followed them from town to town. The
old men, who knew all about evil *windigos* — monster beings —
understood at once that English commander Ralph Lane was
one of them. He was not human; his brutality proved it. The
autumn, too, had been frightening, for the worst drought in
eight hundred years had come in with the English. Corn withered, leaving only wild roots for the Secotan to dig — tasteless
things, of the kind eaten only to survive. Lane didn't plant and

he didn't gather. Instead, he built a fort on Roanoke Island, seized flour and seed corn from the Secotan, ate their pet dogs that strayed into the fort, kidnapped the son of a neighboring chief, abused the boy's crippled father, and shot anyone who resisted.

The year was a year of horror. Lane came to Roanoke: demanding, taking, killing.

How different it had been before. . . .

It had been a warm summer day in 1584 when the English first came ashore. On the fourth of July, two vessels, sent out by Sir Walter Raleigh and commanded by captains Amadas and Barlowe, picked their way along the shoals. Guiding them was a Portuguese pilot named Simon Fernandez. For 120 miles, they had sailed up the coast along a fringe of barrier islands without finding any way to pass between them, while a tense crew shouted depth readings to Fernandez. The ships twisted and turned through the treacherous shallows. The men watched fearfully, well aware of the danger. In later years, this "Skeleton Coast" would drag thousands of ships to their watery graves.

At last Fernandez located a channel. The ships surged in, nearly wrecking, and the shaken sailors suddenly found themselves in the smooth waters of "another great sea" dotted with sandy islands. The ships anchored near a small cove off an island called Hatorask. No one aboard had ever been there before. Yet they had chosen this spot with care. Without ever having seen it, they knew beforehand that this was the place.

And such beauty! The explorers had not expected this. Nothing in Europe had prepared them for the sight of trees so massive, or a landscape so rich. Landing on the beach, the Englishmen scrambled up sand hills, over grapevines that tumbled like ropes from the trees, spilling so many grapes onto the ground that "the very beating and surge of the sea overflowed with them, as were incredible to be written." Incredible indeed! The men laughed out loud, intoxicated by the sights and smells. Loblolly pine and cedar perfumed the air as sweetly as "some delicate garden" abounding with flowers. The explorers stood on the brink of a valley and fired their guns in exhilaration, startling a flock of white cranes, which "arose under us with such a cry, redoubled by many echoes, as if an army of men had shouted all together." Raleigh's men called the Secotan country paradise.

And so it was.

Sandhill cranes like these were often seen by Raleigh's men on Roanoke Island.

When Raleigh's men went exploring, they took an artist along. That person was supposed to "drawe to life one of each kinde of thing that is strange to us in England." John White was the artist Raleigh chose. He drew animals, plants, fish, and people. He recorded the customs of the Secotan, such as dances and feasts. And he drew maps. The sketches of John White are the best source of information we have about the people who lived on Roanoke Island.

This drawing is the first of many of his that you will see in this book. John White drew this picture of Secotan people fishing in the evening in a shallow bay. Light from the fire inside the canoe attracted the fish.

The manner of their fishing.

Two days later, the Secotan made their appearance for the first time. They gathered on the beach, motioning for the explorers to approach, "never making any show of fear or doubt." Barlowe and several others rowed to shore and met them. One was clearly an ambassador, Barlowe noted, for he did all the talking, though he spoke "many things not understood by us." The English gave him a shirt and a hat as a present. In return, he fished for them, taking his canoe into the sound and in less than half an hour completely filling his boat with fish. On shore, he neatly divided the catch into two piles and, pointing first to one ship and then the other, departed. The story later awed listeners in London, who could not imagine such abundance. In truth, the Secotan man's incredible speed makes it

The Secotan ate fresh fish and dried them for winter use.
WATERCOLOR BY JOHN WHITE.

likely that he simply emptied a fishing weir. The English saw nets strung all along the shallow water.

Over the next several days, there were other visits. Large numbers of Secotan came down to the ships, and without ever having to row ashore, the explorers began to know the country, learning the names of people and places. The "king," they were told — describing the situation in the only way they could, by comparing it to their knowledge of English kings and queens — was named Wingina. He was also called Pemisapan. Barlowe soon understood that he was both leader and holy man, and was impressed by the reverence shown to his family. Whenever his brother Granganimeo visited the ships, forty or fifty men accompanied him in state, unrolling a mat upon the sand so that he could sit, and showing him respectful attention. Granganimeo's children often came with him, and so did his wife, who was attended by forty or fifty women. Barlowe thought her bashful, yet very pretty. She went barefoot (it was far too hot in the Secotan country for shoes, and the sand was soft underfoot) and wore a leather dress, with a band of white shells or pearls — he wasn't sure which — around her fore-head. Pearl earrings hung in graceful loops to her waist. Her children wore earrings of copper, and Granganimeo's hair was decorated with a broad plate of the same shining metal.

After this, Barlowe gave up trying to describe anyone, for the shore teemed with people coming to trade. The Secotan indeed showed no fear. Their borders were surrounded by many nations. They were used to foreigners.

By signs, Barlowe learned that the capital of the country was Secota. Later, when he understood the language, he learned

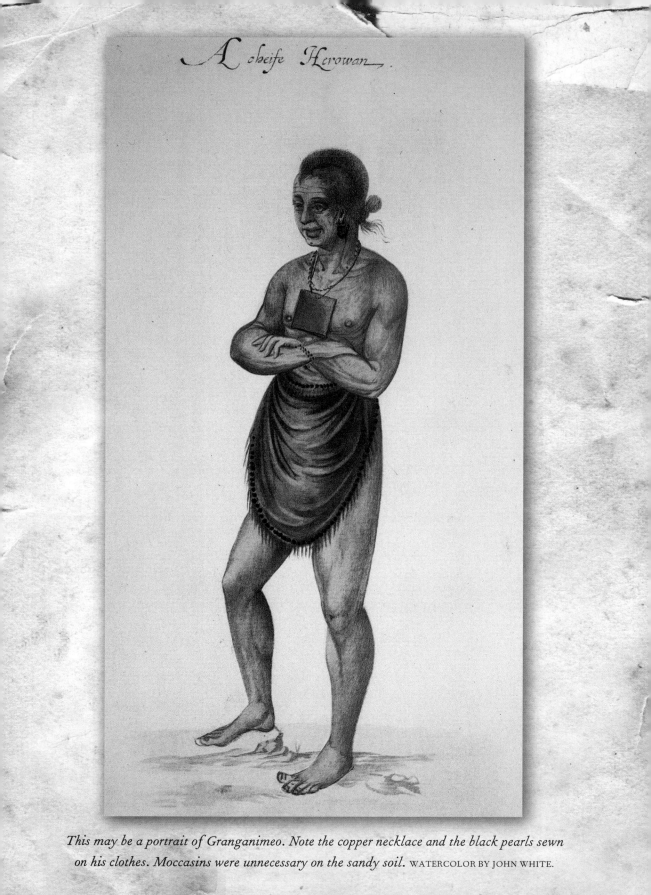

A cheife Herowan

This may be a portrait of Granganimeo. Note the copper necklace and the black pearls sewn on his clothes. Moccasins were unnecessary on the sandy soil. WATERCOLOR BY JOHN WHITE.

more: that Pemisapan had been at Secota during their visit, recovering from battle wounds. He had fought with the leader of a neighboring country and had been shot three times by arrows. Strangely, neither Barlowe nor Amadas thought to ask more about this conflict. Had they paid better attention to the clues, they would have known that something was seriously

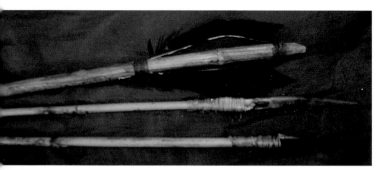

Secotan arrows like these were made of reeds and tipped with birds' beaks. The feathers are turkey.

wrong. When the Secotan traded with the English, what they wanted most were items used for war.

In time, the English would learn that to the north of the Secotan were two other nations, the Weapemeoc and the Chowanoc. Both were related to the Secotan, and were their closest friends. The Chowanoc leader's name was Menatonon. He was unable to use his legs, but this didn't stop him from heading the largest and strongest nation of the three.

In the dark forest to the west lived the Mandoag, a people who were greatly feared. The Mandoag fought well and guarded the trails and rivers through their land so thoroughly that the Secotan did not travel west of their own border. Menatonon's son had once been kidnapped by the Mandoag and escaped. He was one of the few who could describe the country. The reason the Mandoag acted as they did was also well known, for the paths through their country led to the great mine of Chaunis Temoatan, from which came the glittering copper that the Secotan wore.

Raleigh's men noted these facts, but paid them little attention. They had their own interests. It wasn't battles or foreigners or fish or copper they wanted to find . . . but Roanoke, the island of white shell beads. Granganimeo lived there, and from him they learned that it lay in a shallow bay somewhere to the north. It was a place of great beauty. It was a place of mystery.

Days later, they visited Roanoke. Sheltered between the swamp forests to the west and the barrier islands that held back the churning Atlantic Ocean to the east, the island lay in placid water, so narrow one could easily walk across it, so small that one could canoe around it in a single day. Roanoke was stillness. It was shadow that played across sand hills and over tidal creeks. Barlowe knew when he saw it that it was the kind of hidden place he had been instructed to find. It was exactly as he hoped it would be.

At Roanoke Island, Barlowe's boat

The smaller flat beads in this picture are roanoke, which the Secotan made out of whelk shells.

He woemé of Secotam are of Reaſonable good proportion. In their goinge they carrye their hâds danglinge downe, and air dadil in a deer skinne verye excellétlye wel dreſſed, hanginge downe frô their nauell vnto the mydds of their thighes, which alſo couereth their hynder partz. The reſte of their bodies are all bare. The forr parte of their haire is cutt ſhorte, the reſt is not ouer Longe, thinne, and ſofte, and falling downe about their ſhoulders: They weare a Wrrath about their heads.   Their foreheads, cheeks, chynne, armes and leggs are pownced.   About their necks they wear a chaine, ether pricked or paynted. They haue ſmall eyes, plaine and flatt noſes, narrow foreheads, and broade mowths.   For the moſt parte they hange at their eares chaynes of longe Pearles, and of ſome ſmootth bones. Yet their nayles are not longe, as the woemen of Florida.   They are alſo deligtted with walkinge in to the fields, and beſides the riuers, to ſee the huntinge of deers and catchinge of fiſche.

A Secotan woman posed front and back. The words, most likely written by expedition scientist Thomas Hariot, describe her manner and clothes.   BY JOHN WHITE.

was drawn up onto the sand, and Granganimeo's wife "came running out to meet us very cheerfully and friendly." She led the men up a sandy path to a group of cedar houses and invited them into the largest: half home, half statehouse, where visitors were fed and put up for the night. She seated them around a fire that blazed in the middle of the room, despite the summer heat.

What happened next may have been a way of showing hospitality, or perhaps the men were none too clean, or both. Granganimeo's wife washed their garments, including their stockings, while water was brought to bathe their feet. When their clothing was dry, the men were ushered into an inner room bigger than the first. Wide benches lined the walls, and upon these were laid "wooden platters of sweet timber," filled with food: corn mush and roasted deer, fish cooked three different ways, squash, and raspberries. The men ate hungrily, raving over the unfamiliar flavors. Soup, simmered in a white clay pot, was "very sweet and savory." Barlowe was especially intrigued by the herbal tea. He had never had it before, and did not even know what to call it, for the drink had not yet entered England from China.

Secotan pots were pointed at the bottom, similar to this Rappahannock pot from Virginia.

English high tea with its wonderful finger sandwiches and cakes was still in the future, and Barlowe had trouble describing the beverage: "they drink water, but it is sodden" — steeped with "wholesome and medicinal herbs and trees." Wild ginger. Sassafras. Magnolia bark, which tasted like cinnamon.

That evening, as a summer thunderstorm rolled in, the Englishmen departed. Granganimeo's wife sent them away with another meal, which was handed into their boat, "pots and all," along with beautifully woven "mats to cover us from the rain." Barlowe left Roanoke awed by the Secotan. "A more kind and loving people," he wrote in his journal, "cannot be found in the world." All this he recorded, and more; then after a month's stay, the explorers sailed back to Europe. They had seen what they had hoped to find.

CHAPTER 2

Raleigh

At Whitehall Palace in London, Walter Raleigh was Queen Elizabeth's favorite and therefore a celebrity. He was dashing, handsome, and energetic. The queen flirted and laughed with him, gave him a mansion along the Thames and rooms in the palace, and granted him the right to explore and settle the New World. As with any celebrity, the public clamored for details about his life: A green velvet spread trimmed with lace covered his bed; his dinner plates were pure silver; he wore a Secotan pearl earring in one ear; he dressed flamboyantly — rubies, pearls, and diamonds were sewn onto his clothing, and even onto his shoes.

But most remarkable was Raleigh's nimble mind. His wit flashed with meteoric brilliance: He was a bold thinker, a poet, an adventurer, and an inventor. Raleigh was knighted

by the queen; he was her heroic defender.

She needed him. Spain's armies were marching across Europe in a holocaust of invasion and massacre. One by one, nations fell, and England prepared for battle. Assassination attempts against Queen Elizabeth mounted into the hundreds. In London streets, people spoke of war and calamity and omens. No one knew how to break Spain's power. Their military was the best in the world.

Yet Spain's weak point was gold. Its war machine was funded by New World riches: Stop the flow of gold and stop

Top: Queen Elizabeth spoke 7 languages, and spent hours every day reading history.

Bottom: Sir Walter Raleigh's tremendous wit delighted the queen. She nicknamed him "Water," poking fun at his West country pronunciation of "Walter."

Many of King Phillip's galleons (ships) never made it home to Spain, but were captured by English and French pirates or sank to the bottom of the ocean, full of gold, during Caribbean hurricanes.

Spain's power. From the West Country of England, hundreds of boats took to the sea to rob Spanish ships and defend the queen. Merchantmen — designed to carry crates and barrels — were converted into men-of-war and manned by crews who were, said Spain, "good sailors and better pirates — cunning, treacherous and thievish." The pirate ships rode the ocean swells, bearing fearful names: *Seadragon, Black Dog, Dreadnought, Defiance.*

Spanish gold was not the only cargo seized. So much sugar was taken from Spain's South American ships that England came up with a whole new method of eating, spooning sweeteners into food and drink. New desserts and pastries were invented each day.

Spain soon changed the way it sailed. Ships no longer crossed the ocean alone, but in huge convoys, protected by heavily armed warships. Every year, on a day chosen sometime between March and June, the treasure ships gathered in Cuba from all over the Americas. From there, they moved north into the Straits of Florida in powerful formation before randomly sailing a zigzag course across the Atlantic to fool their pursuers. The stratagem worked. England seized fewer Spanish ships, and the queen began to lose ground. Spain, however, had not counted on Raleigh.

The hit-or-miss piracy of the past no longer worked, and Raleigh came up with a far bolder plan. He would build a fort near the Gulf Stream and attack the treasure fleets as they sailed up from Florida before they headed across the ocean. The fort had to be easy to defend, but hard to find. Indeed, it had to be invisible to Spain. This was why, in 1584, Raleigh secretly sent Amadas and Barlowe to America to find such a place. They picked Roanoke, an island hidden from the world. Raleigh would shuttle soldiers to it — not to build a colony, but a military base. When the treasure ships passed, his soldiers would rush from it onto the sea, and Spain's gold would fall into Queen Elizabeth's hands. It was the surest way to save England.

CHAPTER 3
Pemisapan

Raleigh's men returned to the Secotan country the next summer, in the year 1585. Their purpose was to build the fort. Sir Richard Grenville, Raleigh's cousin, led the expedition . . . and with him went Ralph Lane. The two men were bitter enemies. They were too different. Grenville welcomed the Secotans' friendship while Lane, in his turn, killed them.

It was a hot day on June 16, 1585, when Grenville's ships landed at Wococon, a barrier island south of Hatorask. With him were two Secotan men, Manteo and Wanchese, who had gone to London with Amadas and Barlowe as ambassadors for their people, and were now returning home. In London, they had shared the same experiences: They had been wined and dined at Whitehall Palace, dressed in English taffeta clothes, and lodged in Sir Walter Raleigh's mansion. They had been treated kindly and had been taken to plays and masquerade balls. But beyond the glitter of the court, they also saw bears torn to pieces in bear-baiting rings, for money. They saw beggars, robbers, and thieves (among them even children). They saw the Thames River overfished for profit, and masses of people filling the streets and alleys and crowding tenement houses, for England's population had exploded out of control.

England's population explosion let to the exploration of North America and the eventual taking of Indian land.

People had dozens of children until there were simply too many people to fit on the land. A crisis was looming. Wanchese returned to his homeland having seen too much. Manteo, in contrast, would return to England once again. Perhaps he liked it there, or perhaps he was still acting as ambassador.

In an open boat fitted with an awning, Grenville's party rowed to the mainland, visiting town after town. The first they came to was Pomeioc, nestled at the edge of a vast forest of cypress, tupelo, gum, and loblolly pine. The Secotan crowded the shore in greeting. "They are clothed with loose mantles

Their rype corne.

Their greene corne.

Corne newly sprong.

Their sitting at meate.

The place of solemne Prayer.

The house wher'in the Tombe of their Herounds standeth.

SECOTON.

A Ceremony in their prayers w strange iestures and songes danfing abowt posts carued on the topps lyke mens faces.

The capital of Secota was where many villagers flocked for the big summer green corn celebration. Its fields of corn were planted to ripen at different times. WATERCOLOR BY JOHN WHITE.

She manner of their attire and
painting them selues when
they goe to their generall
huntings, or at theire
Solemne feasts.

A cheife Herowans wyfe of Pomeoc.
and her daughter of the age of 8. or.
10. yeares.

Above: a Secotan man painted for the
festival at the capital.
Right: the Pomeioc chief's wife and
daughter. Note the girl's English
baby doll. The gourd in her mother's
hand is for carrying water.

WATERCOLORS BY JOHN WHITE.

made of deer skins and aprons of the same," noted expedition scientist Thomas Hariot. As for their kindness, he agreed with Barlowe. "To confess a truth," he said, "I cannot remember that ever I saw a better or quieter people."

This is believed to be a portrait of scientist Thomas Hariot.

The Secotan guided the men through the trees to their town. Shafts of sunlight fell onto the forest floor, across tree trunks as broad as five men. Underfoot, the soft pine needles were stained purple from fallen grapes. The land, raved Hariot, was "the goodliest soil under the cope of Heaven."

Children peered hesitantly from doorways as the Englishmen entered Pomeioc. The houses were made of cedar wood, which perfumed the town with its scent. Grenville's men spread a blanket on the ground and laid out fishhooks, beads, bugles, and kettles, which they exchanged for Secotan furs and pearls — but not copper, for the Secotan wouldn't part with that. Both sides were delighted with the trade; each thought they had got a bargain. Expedition artist John White sketched the chief's daughter, an eight-year-old girl, holding a baby doll that her father bought her. "They are greatly delighted with puppets and babes," remarked Hariot, "which were brought out of England."

Hariot, observing everything amid the bustle, found the Secotan "very handsome" and watched as White painted their portraits: men, daubed in red and yellow paint, looking very striking with their copper necklaces sparkling in the sun; women, with graceful blue tattoos winding around their arms and shoulders.

By midday, the heat was intense. Grenville's men wilted in their heavy English clothes. Behind the town shimmered a broad lake as blue as any sapphire, and it must have made them envious to see the Secotan frolic in the water. Even snowy egrets and herons waded in its shallow pools, while the soldiers remained on land, for few Europeans could swim.

Mattamuskeet Lake, which lay behind the town of Pomeioc, is still teeming with bird life.

White and Hariot, at least, were paddled around it in a canoe. White later made two maps of the lake, showing its many coves and streams.

Evening fell at last, bringing a slight breeze. Trade goods were put away and women unrolled mats across the plaza, creating a woven carpet of black and red, tan and orange. As the company gathered to eat, wooden platters were passed around, piled high with savory meats and breads, soups, and stews.

What were John White's thoughts that night, as he lay down to sleep in this Secotan town? Was his heart drawn to the land then, with its warm scents and enveloping nights, and the sound of children's laughter? Alligators prowled the swamp forests, giving off deep croaking growls,

Secotan men and women ate on woven mats on opposite sides of the serving platter. Hariot described the meal here as hominy and deer meat "of very good taste." Most meals were also eaten with bread. WATERCOLOR BY JOHN WHITE.

while a chorus of cicadas and frogs hummed soothingly from the trees. Did John White gaze at the constellations spreading silver glitter across the sky, or at the flashes of heat lightning far across the water? It was a land made for dreamers of beauty.

The next morning, Grenville's expedition headed up the coast to Aquascogoc. Again, the welcome was "most courteous." White hauled out sketch paper and waded into the sea of green corn surrounding the town with its waving tassels of deep maroon. The plant was unknown in England, and White curiously

A llagatto . This being but one moneth old was 3 . foote 4 . ynches in length . and lyue in water.

72

From John White's
sketchbook.
Top: an alligator
hatchling he saw in the
Caribbean. Alligators
also lived in the
Secotan country.
Middle: a Secotan fish
barbecue. The different
kinds of wood used
gave the fish flavor.
Bottom: a type of
grouper.

The broyling of their fish ouer the flame of fier .

Mero .

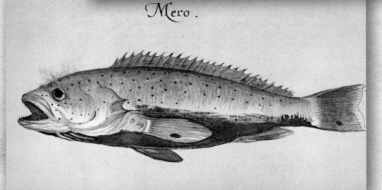

examined the pink, white, and purple cobs. Women pounded the kernels into lavender-tinted flour, molding it into a moist bread called *ponap*. To White, everything was strange and new.

Another day passed all too quickly. Secotan dugouts danced across the water as a crimson sun tumbled into the sound. Fishermen stood upright in them, flinging their nets and hauling them in. Boats came and went in the fading light, their torches twinkling toward land like stars upon the water. At Aquascogoc, everything glowed. Campfires lit up the domed houses with their woven wall patterns, spilling shapes across the sand. Each design was different: stars and birds and fish and kaleidoscopic forms. The Secotan, said Hariot, were "very ingenious."

Toward the end of July, Grenville made ready to return to England. Although his plan had been to remain in the country and build an English fort on Roanoke Island, that changed when he discovered that seawater had entered his ship's cargo and ruined most of their food supply. To Grenville's astonishment, then anger, Lane defiantly announced that he would stay behind with as many soldiers as would follow him, and build the fort anyway. After much heated argument, Lane got his way. He and 107 men were taken to Roanoke, with all the bread and meat Grenville could spare. The ration would not last more than twenty days. Knowing that Grenville could not possibly return with more supplies before spring, Lane was confident the

Secotan would feed them. It was more than military honor that spurred him on. Lane was certain that the Secotan's copper jewelry contained traces of gold, and he imagined the fame that would be his if he found the mine of Chaunis Temoatan.

For the Secotan, Lane's relentless quest would bring ruin.

Trouble began with the rain that did not come. A blistering sun scorched the earth as days turned into weeks, and still no rain fell from the sky. The soil underfoot dried into sand. Gardens, once so bountiful, withered and died. There had been droughts before, but not like this.

Hariot, the scientist, watched the corn shrivel. To try to take the Secotan's mind off their troubles, he showed them magnifying glasses, a spyglass (in which they saw "many strange sights"), fireworks, and windup clocks. These wonders exhausted, he wandered to the outskirts of their towns and surveyed the oak and pine, sweet gum and beech trees, enjoying their shade. Their size was colossal. In England, the largest trees in the forest were always cut first — out of necessity, for wood was scarce. In fact, few forests remained anywhere in the kingdom. Too many people had cut too much until there was almost no fuel left to heat their houses except for peat and dried grasses. The Secotan managed their forests just the opposite, cutting only small saplings for use and letting the mammoth trees expand. Darting under their shade, Secotan children played among giants.

On September 27, a comet blazed through the night sky, startling English and Secotan alike. Both took it as an omen. The next day, the Secotan began to die. Neither side understood how germs spread; neither knew that the Secotan had no resistance to European diseases, even including the common cold. Within "a few days after our departure from every . . . town," wrote Hariot, "the peo-

The corpses of Secotan leaders were embalmed and laid in a mortuary temple like this one at Secota.
DRAWING BY JOHN WHITE.

ple began to die very fast, and many in short space; in some towns about twenty, in some forty, in some sixty, and in one six score. . . . The disease was so strange that they neither knew what it was, nor how to cure it." The oldest men in the country said that nothing like it had ever happened before, "time out of mind."

Granganimeo died. To confront the emergency, his brother, Pemisapan, moved from the capital of Secota to Roanoke. Food shortages caused by the drought soon followed, as Lane bullied his way through the towns, stealing supplies and demanding hostages who could lead him into the Mandoag country. At the Chowanoc capital to the north, Lane seized Menatonon's young son and held him for ransom inside the fort at Roanoke, where the boy was chained and beaten. Caring little about the Secotan's problems, Lane was certain that they were deliberately withholding food from him, and he decided he would teach them a lesson. It was one they would not soon forget.

In a bloodred dawn, Lane's soldiers crept through a canebrake at the edge of the town of Dasamonquepeuc, opposite Roanoke Island, where Pemisapan was staying. The soldiers watched him as he stood outside of his house surrounded by advisers.

Lane may have been mad. He must have been *windigo*, for he had made Pemisapan his enemy when they could have been friends. Surely this is what the old men said. After this they said no more, for Lane and his troops were upon them. Pemisapan saw the English commander's mouth open in a single bloodcurdling scream: "Christ our victory!" At the signal, the soldiers' weapons flashed, belching flame and smoke into the town. Secotan women and children fled in all directions, wailing, crying out against the troops. Bodies crumpled to the earth, and in one awful moment, Pemisapan's head was struck off with a sword.

This happened on the first of June, 1586.

CHAPTER 4
London

In London, far from Ralph Lane's massacre, John White perfected his portraits. An artist of enormous talent and insight, he was a master at watercolors, and as he applied pinks and golds and blues to paper, the Secotan country came alive. He had been on both of Raleigh's voyages — with Barlowe and Grenville — as expedition artist. When White's paintings were finished, Raleigh would present them to the queen.

How impressed she would be! Few could draw natural history the way White did, and few places were as vivid and colorful as the route through the Caribbean to the Secotan coast. His pictures of exotic plants and animals were as stunning as the emerald Caribbean Sea: dazzling blue fins on a dolphin fish, hot-pink flamingos, a soft buttery banana. Purple streamers on a Portuguese man-of-war. A golden pineapple. A hermit crab.

This is a lyuing fish, and flote vpon the Sea, Some call them Caruels

Duratho. Of thes some a

Caracol.

A Flaminco.

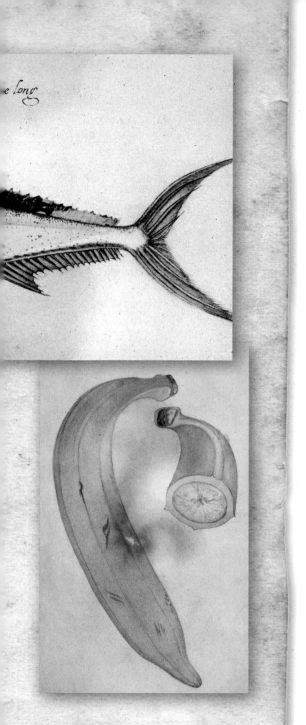

e long

John White's drawings, clockwise from top left: Poutuguese man-of-war; dolphin fish; banana; flamingo; hermit crab; pineapple (called "pine fruit" because of its resemblance to a pinecone).

It had been summer each time White visited the Secotan country, with its hauntingly beautiful forests and coastline. In place of London's noise and confusion, vast swamp forests echoed the sounds of the whip-poor-will and wood thrush. Instead of teeming slums and markets whose streets ran with human sewage and the guts and gore from butcher shops, White found secluded bays, peaceful villages, and clean, windswept beaches. He must have fallen in love with the place, for he went back again and again.

As yet we know little about White himself. He was forty-five years old and married when he visited Roanoke, though his wife may not have been alive. Women often died in childbirth, as she may have done. The couple had a daughter, Eleanor, who was nineteen the summer of Lane's massacre. She was married to a bricklayer named Ananias Dare. We know that White was born in Ireland and was educated, as his fine handwriting and his way with words shows. Where he learned to paint and how he came to be part of the Roanoke expeditions is not yet fully known. We know White mostly through his drawings, and through the heart-wrenching letters he left behind.

John White was certainly familiar with London. Whitehall, the queen's residence west of the London gate, was the largest palace in Europe. Tourists flocked by the hundreds to see it. Under its roof lived 1500 courtiers and staff with enormous

The court of Queen Elizabeth I. Raleigh is the man on the far left.

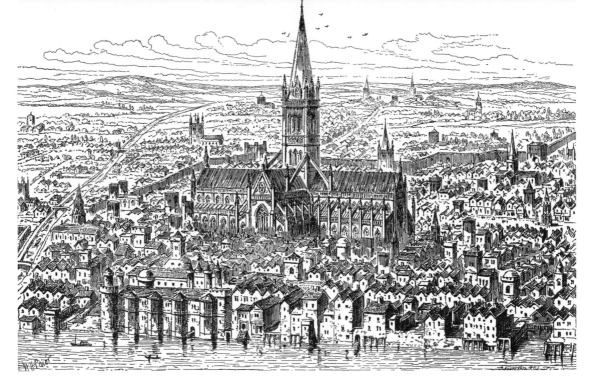

A bird's-eye view of London showing its graceful buildings —
and also its extreme crowding.

appetites, who each year gobbled up 33,024 chickens, 13,260 lambs, 8,200 sheep, 1,240 head of beef, 2,500 tons of ale, and 60,000 pounds of butter.

No city in England boasted more craftsmen than London. Shops offered gloves, hats, perfumes, soap, saddles, needles, linens, cheese, toys, and scores of other items. Downstream from the palace, butchers' stalls lined the Thames River, selling more meat in a single day than the citizens of Portugal ate in an entire year. Wherries, padded with cushions, ferried people up and down the river, taking them to London's main attractions. The top tourist spots were Saint Paul's Cathedral, surrounded by a courtyard filled with booksellers' carts (a favorite haunt

London Bridge, under its row of shops. Raleigh's house and
Whitehall palace were just upriver to the left.

for pickpockets and thieves); the fearsome Tower of London, a
state prison where visitors could view its tormented inmates
along with caged lions and tigers; and London Bridge, smoth-
ered by a row of elegant stores that had been built right on top
of it. The bridge even boasted a live camel — visitors loved
it! — tied to a merchant's door.

Fads were always popular in London. Young people were
fond of dancing, though the new steps were considered quite
shocking. No less bizarre were the ever-changing clothing
styles. Ladies at court wore farthingale dresses, hooped with

whalebone and draped with a staggering twenty yards of cloth. Queen Elizabeth's gowns were just as full, studded with pearls and precious gems. One garment glittered with 365 diamonds, one for each day of the year. For men, short French breeches were in style, and were much ridiculed by the older generation. Nothing could look

Although gowns and doublets were hot and uncomfortable, Queen Elizabeth and friends enjoyed picnicking outdoors.

stranger than these pants, grumbled William Harrison, unless "it were a dog in a doublet." Philip Stubbes thought doublets themselves were "monstrous," being padded and stuffed so thickly that men could "hardly either stoop down or decline themselves."

So outlandish were the fashions that laws were passed defining appropriate clothing styles for each class. But the laws couldn't stop Londoners from competing in other ways: in the kinds of foods served or dishware displayed, in writing poetry, playing musical instruments, or even owning pets. Women clamored over small dogs, parading them out in the streets to the envy of every passerby. A popular saying in London was "Love me, love my dog."

Where did John White fit into London with its changing styles and social classes? Was he wealthy? He had a coat of arms suggesting that he might be. Was he religious? His letters seem to point that way, for in each of them, he never failed to mention God. We do know that White was interested in travel and painted foreign visitors who came to town.

Perhaps the most that we know about White is that he appears to have had nothing to do with Raleigh's military plan. The Roanoke fort was not his concern. Instead, he had a different vision: to create a utopia, a peaceful community of colonists, far from the turmoil of Europe and far from Lane's ravages at Roanoke. Raleigh approved of the project, and gave White permission and ships and money to make it happen. White himself would be the colony's governor. From the Secotan, he had heard of the Chesapeake Bay, ninety miles to the north of Roanoke in the territory of the Powhatan. To solve the mystery of the Lost Colony, it is important to know White's plans. White intended to go to Chesapeake Bay, not Roanoke Island. With his family and closest friends, he would build a settlement in freedom and security, in friendship with the Powhatan. Nothing quite like it had ever been tried before. He would call his town the City of Raleigh.

It was a wonderful dream.

CHAPTER 5
The Voyage

May 8, 1587. On the deck of a ship called the *Lion*, John White, his daughter, Eleanor (who was six months pregnant), and her husband, Ananias, bade farewell to Plymouth harbor. Their convoy was small: divided between two ships were 117 men, women, and children, nearly all of them White's friends. Of their history we know nothing, except for their names and the fact that many seem to have been wealthy. A third vessel carried supplies: bedding, clothing, pans, pillows, tools, ink, and glue — everything they would need to begin a new life along the Chesapeake Bay, except for food. They would buy this in the Caribbean islands that lay along their route.

Gulls shrieked around billowing sails as the ships eased out of the harbor. Children clung to the railing, straining for one last look at Plymouth, with its whitewashed shops filled with creams and pastries, wax dolls and whistles, its cobbled streets thronging with merchants, sailors, dogs, and carts.

They would never see these things again. Nor would their parents ever behold the loved ones they were leaving behind, for they themselves would never return. Something had gone wrong. From the moment they boarded the ships, the colonists were in trouble. How many of them knew this? How many guessed what lay ahead? If they did not recognize the danger already, it would become clear as the journey progressed.

The first mishap occurred off the Portuguese coast. It appeared to be an accident, but it was not. The smaller ship, commanded by Captain Spicer and carrying part of the company, was left behind in the middle of the night. These were dangerous enemy waters, controlled by Spain — English sailors and travelers captured by Spain might be imprisoned or burned at the stake. Simon Fernandez, the captain of White's

vessel, refused to search for the missing ship, or to wait. The separation was a dreadful blow. Half the colonists were lost, and days of tension followed as the others worried over the fate of their friends. This accident, which was no accident, was number one. Nine more soon followed.

The Virgin Islands are made up of 50 small islands that are famous for their beauty.

June 22. The ships reached the Virgin Islands in the Caribbean, and the colonists went ashore. After weeks at sea, its lush lagoons and tropical breezes were luxuriously refreshing. Fernandez was a licensed ship's pilot and an expert in these islands. His survival skills included knowledge of the region's exotic plants. Someone showed the colonists a green fruit and said it was edible. Was it Fernandez? They ate, and were instantly struck down, mouths burning, tongues

The Lost Colonists' last view of England was of this shore surrounding the harbor in Plymouth, England. It still looks much as it did in 1587 when White's colonists sailed from here to Roanoke.

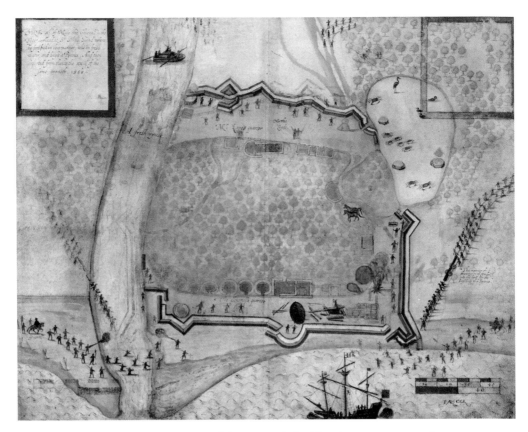

John White's drawing of the Spanish fortifications on Puerto Rico.

swelling into their throats. Luckily, no one died. Poisonous fruit — accident number two.

Fresh streams flowed through the Virgin Islands, tumbling into pools, but the colonists were never taken to any, despite their asking for them. Instead, they were led to a contaminated pond they were told was safe and at once "fell sick with drinking thereof." Not just a little sick, but life-threateningly so. Those who only washed their faces in the water found their skin on fire, burning and puffing out to such an extent that "their eyes were shut up." They were blind for nearly a week. Poisonous water — accident number three.

White's dream for the City of Raleigh was dying.

As complaints mounted, Fernandez directed the ships to Puerto Rico, where he promised fresh water, though again they found none. Here, too, White was supposed to gather salt, which the colonists needed if they hoped to preserve food for the coming winter until supply ships arrived. Yet Fernandez would not allow it, pretending there was "great danger" from shallow water, though he had sailed to the salt banks many times before. Every Roanoke expedition had stopped there; the only one that didn't was John White's. Nor were they allowed to gather plants that they had hoped to cultivate — accidents number four and number five.

In fact, Fernandez had gone to Puerto Rico for only one reason. The island was Spanish territory, and it was there that one of the company ran away. His name was Darby Glande, and he claimed never to have been a colonist at all. He had been kidnapped and forced aboard ship, he said, then released on Puerto Rico. To save his life after he fell into Spanish hands, Glande talked — as someone knew he would — alerting authorities to White's planned settlement. Strangely, he said this would be on Roanoke Island, not at the Chesapeake Bay. What did Glande know? Who told him to say this? The answers will soon become clear, but this much is certain: As a result of his statement, Spain launched an expedition to search for White's colony and destroy it — "accident" number six.

By now, the ships were halfway across the Caribbean, and no supplies had been collected. At Hispaniola, where cattle and other provisions were to be bought, Fernandez refused to land. At last, openly vowing that he would stop nowhere, he sailed to the North Carolina coast and allowed the ships to drift. Accident number seven. Accident number eight. Days passed, until it was too late in the summer to plant. The colonists would harvest no food.

Eight accidents. Half the company lost, no water, no rations, no salt, no planting, and Spain notified of their location. Two pregnant women were aboard ship as well as a small baby; their needs were ignored. Drinking water had become stinking and slimy. Food was stale. Human waste and rotten garbage dribbled into the space belowdecks, creating a putrid smell. The truth was now unmistakable: Fernandez had sabotaged them, though White could not know why.

The worst was yet to come. Accident number nine, the most deadly of all: White's company never reached the Chesapeake Bay. Against their wishes, Fernandez marooned them on Roanoke Island.

CHAPTER 6
Mutiny

It was mutiny, pure and simple. Fernandez landed White's colonists at Roanoke and ordered the sailors to "leave them in the island." In desperation, White pleaded that the planters be taken the remaining ninety miles to the Chesapeake Bay. Fernandez refused. The summer was too far gone to waste the time, he said — then spent a month at Roanoke leisurely recaulking his ships.

Few places were more dangerous during that summer of 1587 than Roanoke Island. Fernandez knew this. The Secotan country was in shambles, its leader murdered by Lane, its survivors still struggling with the aftermath of starvation, sickness, and death. Englishmen could not have been welcome. And indeed, they were not. On Roanoke Island, White stumbled upon the bleached bones of a soldier who had been left to man the fort after Lane's troops withdrew. The fourteen others who had been posted with him were gone. They had been White's last hope. His colonists had reached the end: There would be no help from the fort. Its buildings lay in ruins. No soldiers' supply ships would come to save them. Fernandez would tell the queen that the troops were all dead.

White did what he could, ordering repairs made to Lane's houses, which had become overgrown with weeds and vines. New houses were built to shelter everyone. And shock settled in. A numbness. For this was Roanoke. They would not survive.

August 25. Spicer's ship, abandoned in Spanish waters, miraculously found its way to Roanoke Island, though the captain had never been there before. The missing colonists were rowed ashore "to the great joy and comfort of the whole company." Yet the happiness did not last long. It would have been better if Spicer had not tried to find them, and instead had returned them to England. The colonists he carried had escaped capture by Spain . . . only to be marooned along with the rest.

In the days that followed, White's company gathered what food they could. Leaving his young son, George Howe Jr., behind, George Howe waded alone into the sound to hunt crabs. He was later discovered facedown in the water, with sixteen Secotan arrows sticking out of his back. Was it White who had to tell the boy what had happened? Lane had murdered Pemisapan. The colonists, who were innocent, would pay heavily for his crimes . . . and someone in England would let them.

In despair, White led a delegation to the Secotan town on the island of Croatoan, where Manteo was born. With him was Manteo himself, who had gone to England with Lane after the massacre. White brought him home: Manteo was his only link to the country. To White's relief, the people of Croatoan welcomed them kindly. Yet White could not ignore the scars that he saw from Lane's war: a man paralyzed by gunfire, scanty food supplies, tension, and fear. The Croatoans could not feed White's colonists; they could scarcely feed themselves. George Howe and the soldier at the fort, they told him, had been killed by Wanchese and others who had survived Lane's massacre at Dasamonqueqeuc. The fourteen remaining soldiers had fled to the sea in their boat. They were never seen again.

What were White's emotions then? Croatoan's weakness could only have made him feel more alone. Manteo's people could not help him; the colonists were cut off from the world. White's fears were calmed only by the kindness of Manteo's people. They gave him that, though they could give no more. White returned their generosity, vowing to keep "the old love that was between us," and live together "as brethren and friends." The Croatoans agreed to take his message of peace to the other Secotan towns. Yet too much misery had passed. They could make no promises.

John White understood the danger. He and his colonists were alone in a killing field far from England, while anchored offshore were the ships that could have taken them to the Chesapeake Bay and away from all that — before Fernandez betrayed them.

Eight days later, it happened again. Just before dawn, Edward Stafford, captain of the supply ship, led an attack on Dasamonquepeuc, where peace talks between the colonists and the Secotan were to have taken place. The only arrivals were White's friends from Croatoan, who were fired upon while seated around a campfire. The "miserable souls," White moaned, "herewith amazed, fled to a place of thick reeds, where our men shot one of them through the body with a bullet." The only help the colonists might have hoped to get from the Secotan was gone. "Accident" number ten.

August 18, a moment of happiness amid the distress. White's daughter, Eleanor, gave birth to a baby girl and named her Virginia Dare. She was the first English child born in America. Her christening took place at the water's edge. Had it been on the shore of the Chesapeake Bay, how happy all would have been! Instead, the celebration ended abruptly: Word came that

An artist's fanciful drawing of the baptism of Virginia Dare.
In reality White, not a priest, baptized the child, and the baptism
took place outside. No building this big existed at Roanoke.

the ships were leaving. The moment had arrived when the colonists would be stranded. In renewed panic, they begged White to try to go to England for help. No one less than the governor of the colony would be believed. Their tale was too strange — they were accusing Fernandez of mutiny and murder.

Curiously, Fernandez agreed to let White return, though

punishment for the crime of mutiny was death. His willingness to risk this meant that Fernandez had a protector. Someone knew he had sabotaged White's colony, and had approved it. But why did Fernandez do it? Why did he want the colonists dead? Or did he? What if his protector had ordered it? If so, John White must have known that somewhere in England was a powerful and dangerous enemy . . . who would make sure his story was not believed.

CHAPTER 7
Enemies

The parting came too fast. One moment John White was with his family and the friends he loved most in the world; in the next, in crippling sorrow, with tears and regrets, in sickening fear, he abandoned them. He left them standing on the beach as he climbed into the boat that would take him away. He left them, marooned on an island in a land that Lane had destroyed. Through Darby Glande, Spain had been warned of their location. No one could protect them: The soldiers were gone. No supply ships would come. And gripping White's heart was the awful knowledge that no one would believe him. Could he get help? Would it come in time?

In the final moments before he was rowed to Spicer's ship, White had instructed the colonists to carve on the trees or door-posts of the houses the name of their destination if they left the island. He then gave them an important secret sign: "I willed them," he said, "that if they should happen to be distressed, they should carve over the letters or name a cross," like this: +. Again and again, he made them promise to do this.

On the morning of August 27, 1587, White left them and sailed away.

Time was critical. White's only hope of saving his colonists was in beating Fernandez home and telling Raleigh his story first. Yet halfway across the Atlantic, the trade winds disappeared. The ship lay motionless upon the sea until supplies dwindled and there were only three gallons of water left for all of the crew. White prayed for wind, and it came in a ferocious blast — a wild, pelting storm that drove the ship far off course. The sailors sickened, then died.

October 16. Spicer's ship drifted quietly onto the Irish coast, a ghost ship upon the water. The villagers of Smerwick, knowing what to do, rushed aboard with water and medicines. White and Captain Spicer were rowed ashore. Somehow, White summoned the strength, weak as he was, to search the harbor for a ship to England, but there was none. Frantically, he begged captain after captain, but every answer was the same. Borrowing a horse, he thundered along the coast to other towns, each mile

Spicer's small boat, which carried White home, had a crew of 15.
During the voyage, 2 died and all but 5 were too sick to stand.

pounding into his soul, for he was no closer to saving his colonists than he had been when he first left Roanoke so many weeks
before. No ships. No way home.

November 1. Two weeks after his arrival in Ireland, White
at last found a sluggish vessel bound for Southampton and took
it, reaching England after an entire week of sailing. In London,
he learned that Fernandez and Stafford had beat him back by
nearly a month. Both had announced the arrival of the colonists
"at their wished haven" — the Chesapeake Bay. A book had
even been rushed into print celebrating the happy event.

Everywhere, people were jubilant that England's first colony in America was a success. White alone knew the truth: On Roanoke, the colonists would not survive the winter.

At Durham House, in his favorite room that overlooked the Thames, Raleigh listened in shock to White's story. He responded immediately. Ordering a ship and supplies, he hurried to his desk and wrote a letter to the colonists, promising that a whole fleet would be sent to them in the spring. Meanwhile, the supply ship would leave at once, despite the danger. It was the first time the English had ever attempted a winter crossing of the Atlantic Ocean. The colonists' plight was worth the risk.

There is no evidence that Raleigh's ship ever left the harbor. At the time of Stafford's return to London in October, the Council of Shipping and Mariners ordered all vessels confined to port. The reason given was the impending war with Spain, yet the council

Profits from his Viginia colony made Sir Walter the richest man in the kingdom.

knew that the Spaniards would not come that year. Their warships had been destroyed months before in a stinging attack on them made by England's Sir Francis Drake. There was no war threat that October. Who ordered the stay?

Raleigh and White must have discussed this. Indeed, they must have been frantic to put a name to the faceless enemy who had condemned 116 innocent people to death on Roanoke Island. Was it someone with a hatred of the colonists? If so, what had they done? We know little about them, but if someone did not like who they were or what they stood for, weren't they leaving the country? Didn't that solve the problem? Why sabotage them?

There was one possibility, horrible to consider: What if the killer was not after the colonists at all? What if the target was Sir Walter Raleigh? Destroying the colony would ruin Raleigh. In whose way had the bold adventurer stepped?

Raleigh, like other independent freethinkers, had many friends and also many enemies. Palace rivals wished to see him fail. Yet mere hatred of Raleigh could not have pulled off such a sabotage. Power and cunning were also required. Whoever did it, did it well, going so far as to kidnap Darby Glande and release him on a Spanish island to make extra sure the colonists were destroyed. Whoever did it hired Fernandez and was able to protect him from his crimes. Whoever did it had to be certain that the colonists were never rescued. Whoever did it had to prevent the queen from interfering, despite the fact that Raleigh was her favorite. And, finally, whoever did it taught Fernandez to say these words: "The summer was too far spent for planting." The person who was guilty of the crime taught Fernandez to stall.

This is a clue. The sabotage, the excuse — indeed, the exact phrase used — the marooning of colonists had all been done before.

It had happened in 1517, exactly seventy years before the sabotage of White's expedition, when the first English colony to the New World had been planned. The colonists' destination had been Newfoundland. Their governor was John Rastell.

King Henry VIII approved of the colony, just as his daughter, Queen Elizabeth, approved of White's plans. The Earl of Surrey, Lord Admiral of the navy, was an enthusiastic supporter. He funded part of the voyage and even gave his servant, John Ravyn, to Rastell to act as the ship's purser, the officer in charge of the ship's accounts.

But there was something wrong with Rastell's expedition. It had barely begun when Ravyn began stalling. He delayed the ship by not buying supplies, though he promised them at port after port, just as Fernandez had done in the Caribbean. Days slipped away. If Rastell hoped to start his Newfoundland colony before winter set in, he was running out of time. At Plymouth harbor in the south of England, Ravyn drove a hole into the ship, causing more delay while it was repaired. At last, everything was set in order. The supplies were loaded, and the ship finally sailed away from land and into the English Channel. Yet it never got beyond the coast of Ireland, where Ravyn stopped making excuses and openly forced Rastell's colonists off the ship. He marooned them on the island, claiming that the summer was too far spent to take them any farther.

A court trial followed. To everyone's amazement, Ravyn was never put in jail. The Earl of Surrey protected him, admitting that he himself had ordered the sabotage. Despite this shocking confession, the earl was never arrested either; his power and position protected him. Strangely, it was Rastell who took the fall. He became the victim of a smear campaign that accused him of being a poor leader since he was unable to control Ravyn. No one could quite believe that the powerful earl, head of King Henry VIII's navy, would ruin a project (despite his confession) that he had so actively supported.

Who at Queen Elizabeth's court had read these records? Who knew the history of Rastell and Ravyn so well that he could copy the very wording of the sabotage? Someone did. Someone ordered Fernandez to destroy the colonists, and then protected him from arrest. Whoever it was had to be as powerful as the

Earl of Surrey, to make sure no one went to jail. He had to turn people's opinions against White, which was exactly what he did.

Only four men in England in 1587 could have done this. All four were members of the queen's Privy Council. They were her closest advisers. They were: the Earl of Leicester, Sir Christopher Hatton, Lord Burghley, and Sir Francis Walsingham. The question is, which one had the motive, the method, the means, and the opportunity to do it?

Robert Dudley, Earl of Leicester, was certainly a prime suspect. He was Queen Elizabeth's oldest favorite and her most trusted adviser. In the early years of her reign, people fully believed that she would marry Leicester and make him king. She never did. Elizabeth was, however, fond of him, for while new favorites came and went, Leicester stayed.

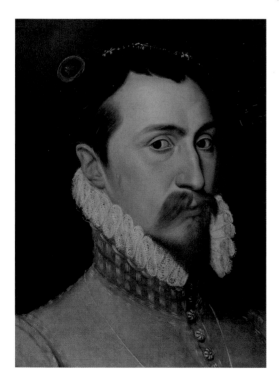

Easygoing with his friends, Leicester could be quite ruthless with enemies. Accused of bribery and even murder, he was reckless

Robert Dudley, Earl of Leicester

*At Leicester's estate at Kenilworth, he lavishly entertained the queen
with elaborate water pagents and spectacular fireworks.*

and bold. Could he have ordered the Roanoke sabotage?
Unlikely. Secrecy was not his style, nor did he have the patience
to carry out such a sabotage. Moreover, Leicester had no motive.
He was wealthy, he was popular, he got on well with the queen.
He and Raleigh, though rivals, had always been friends. Neither
Roanoke nor Raleigh were any threat to Leicester.

Sir Christopher Hatton was another of the queen's favorites. Indeed, his devotion to her was so great he never married.
Perhaps he liked her better than she liked him; he had only

Sir Christopher Hatton

caught her eye because of his fine dancing ability. Unlike Leicester, who was confident of his position at court, Hatton was not. His fear of being pushed aside was well known, and so was his envy of Raleigh. He complained bitterly to the queen that she liked Raleigh better, and she did.

Generally thought of as an honest man, Hatton may have had a dark side. He was believed by many to have murdered a rival. If so, then the Roanoke sabotage wasn't his style either. Whoever had hoped to ruin Raleigh by destroying the colonists was a mastermind whose trademark was secrecy. That person was also indirect, for he did not attack Raleigh. Instead, he ruined the colonists.

Although jealousy might have made Hatton do it, he normally shrank back and complained to the queen rather than take action. His personality didn't fit the Roanoke crime. Furthermore, despite his worries that the queen preferred Raleigh, Hatton continued to do very well at court. He was promoted to greater and richer jobs and became wealthy, though he didn't have much power. Of the four suspects, Hatton is the weakest.

William Cecil, Lord Burghley, was the queen's oldest adviser. A lawyer, he was also her treasurer. If a poll had been taken, everyone in the kingdom would have said he was a genius . . . and also very dull and boring. Burghley worked single-mindedly for the queen and allowed no distractions. He didn't flirt with her and he had no time for jealousy. People wondered if Burghley even had a hobby. Cautious, serious, a workhorse, and powerful, he hired spies to help protect the kingdom.

Burghley certainly had the ability to plan the sabotage, but did he do it? Why would he? He was a professional; he played by the rules. He wasn't jealous of Raleigh's wealth, power, or position, for he had more than Raleigh of all three. His salary was the second highest in the realm, and it was

William Cecil, Lord Burghley

Burghley's magnificent estate of Theobolds stretched a quarter of a mile long. Inside, it was lavish, with fountains and chandeliers.

said that even a king would not be ashamed to live in Burghley's enormous mansion. He was known to be on friendly terms with Raleigh, liked the idea of an American base, and let Raleigh use his grand library whenever he wished. Burghley's flower gardens, which were the talk of England, were tended by none other than botanist John Gerard, a friend of John White's.

We are left with only one suspect: Sir Francis Walsingham, the queen's secretary of state. He and Burghley were the titans of the queen's government, and both had enormous power. Walsingham had more. Slick with words, he was able to talk even foreign kings into doing things his way . . . sometimes without their even knowing it. Leicester's and Hatton's crimes were petty compared to Walsingham's. They may have done away with a political opponent from time to time; he brought down a queen: The entrapment and death of Mary Stuart, queen of Scotland, was largely Walsingham's doing.

Sir Francis Walsingham

He had the biggest spy system in England, far greater than Burghley's. On his payroll were more than five hundred agents, spread throughout the kingdom and across Europe. He was, people said, "a diligent searcher out of hidden secrets and one who knew exactly well how to win men's affections to him and to make use of them for his own purposes."

Among those whose hidden secrets Walsingham discovered was a Portuguese ship's pilot living in England, who had been arrested for piracy. His own government wanted him hanged. Ignoring them, Walsingham used his power and saved the man's life. Did he then use him "for his own purposes"? He must have: After this, the convict Simon Fernandez was known as "Walsingham's man." Simon Fernandez, who marooned White's colonists on Roanoke Island, owed Walsingham a favor.

Could Walsingham have ordered the Roanoke sabotage? Easily. Its careful planning was his trademark. It was how he did things. But why would he do it? What was his motive?

In criminal investigations, police are lucky when they find one motive. Had they been present in 1587 and examined Walsingham's life, they would have found two. Either one might have caused the Roanoke tragedy; with both, the colonists never stood a chance.

For years, as secretary of state, Walsingham had steadily been increasing his control over European kings. With his enormous spy network, he knew all their secrets and carefully plotted move and countermove for every one. For more than ten years, his shrewd eye had been turned on Spain, putting things in place in order to keep England — and himself — one step ahead.

Only Raleigh stood in his way. A brash knight in shining armor, he knew nothing of Walsingham's plans and boldly announced that he would attack Spain himself, from America. The queen liked the idea. Walsingham didn't. He had spent too many years maneuvering Spain where he wanted it, to let Raleigh destroy everything with Roanoke.

The problem was, Raleigh was too successful. He awed the kingdom with everything he did, "in court, camp, by sea, by land, with sword, with pen." As a friend bluntly put it, "He was no slug." A knight, an adventurer, a fighter, a risk taker, a poet! — Raleigh was everything . . . and a loose cannon.

Walsingham had to destroy Spain. He also had to destroy Raleigh.

If detectives had looked for a second motive for the Roanoke crime in 1587, they would have found it easily enough: money.

Despite a lifetime working for the queen, Walsingham had never been Elizabeth's favorite. At times she could barely stand him. He paid for his vast spy network himself, out of his own pocket. No one helped him. Walsingham was not rich like Burghley, nor from a noble family like Leicester. Raleigh, too, was well off, with a mansion and riches, ships, soldiers, and the gift of America, all from the queen. Walsingham had only what he could scrape together.

As Spain geared up for a massive invasion of England, Walsingham's secret service stepped up their activity. His spies were paid well in gold and silver. This, along with family debts, gifts, and loans to foreign diplomats added up to a crisis for Walsingham that summer of 1587. He badly needed money.

The year before, after uncovering a plot against England, he had expected that the wealthy traitors' homes and riches would be given to him by the queen as his reward for saving her life. He never got them. Instead, the queen gave them to Raleigh to fund his Roanoke expeditions! The secretary of state bitterly asked Elizabeth for a loan . . . and was turned down.

For Walsingham, it all led back to Roanoke. In 1583, before Raleigh sent out his first expedition, Walsingham was in London drumming up funds so that his stepson could sail to America. He was well aware that whoever settled the country first would become, overnight, the wealthiest man in the kingdom. He didn't move fast enough. Before Walsingham could raise the money, Queen Elizabeth gave the land to a bold adventurer named Sir Walter Raleigh.

Raleigh had it all. Money. Power. Roanoke. A base from which to destroy Spain. It was said that Walsingham "could overthrow any matter . . . and move it so as it must fall." Only Walsingham was shrewd enough and desperate enough to work out every detail of the Roanoke sabotage, leaving nothing to chance. Only one man in England had the power, the motive, the means, and the opportunity to sabotage 116 innocent people on Roanoke Island and ruin Raleigh's plan. Walsingham did it. And he got away with murder.

CHAPTER 8
Pirates

In the winter of 1588, Raleigh swung into action, readying a fleet of seven ships for the rescue of White's colonists. The vessels were packed with supplies, and perhaps with soldiers, too, for Raleigh had not yet given up the idea of using Roanoke as a military base. By spring, the chilling news reached England that Spain's navy had been rebuilding. Its armada of massive warships was so mighty it was said to be invincible. Its arrival by sea would be as lethal as a swarm of locusts by land. Nothing could stop it.

War was at hand. London's streets swelled with refugees from Europe with horror stories to tell. Prophecies spread like wildfire, predicting "strange and wonderful events for the year." At night, the queen's zodiac sign of Virgo was blotted

Ruins of the Glastonbury Abbey,
hit by the earthquake of 1588.

out by a lunar eclipse, sending shivers of terror across the land. In the west of England, an earthquake rattled down houses and damaged a church. Many believed it was the end of the world.

By March, Raleigh's ships were ready to sail, waiting only for a fair wind before they were put to sea. As White anxiously paced the deck, scanning the clouds for a break in the weather, Walsingham struck again. By order of the Privy Council, Raleigh's Roanoke vessels were seized and given to the navy for the war effort. Yet the navy already had enough ships. Not a single one of Raleigh's was ever used. The Lord Admiral himself filed a lawsuit on Raleigh's behalf, charging that the vessels had been taken needlessly "yet by order from the Council."

By this time, White's colonists had been left alone for seven months, with their food supplies completely gone. How many were still alive? Eleanor? Her baby, Virginia Dare? Ananias?

Those in England who knew of the tragedy began to speak of the colonists as "lost." Sick with disappointment, White made appeal after appeal to the authorities, begging "so earnestly" for his colonists' relief that at last the Privy Council gave him a small ship. The gift was no gift at all. The ship was far too small to cross the ocean alone. White knew it. He went anyway.

April 22, 1588. The thirty-ton *Brave*, carrying John White, set sail from England for Roanoke Island. Fifteen colonists were also aboard. Who were they? Family members, anxious to rejoin their loved ones marooned on Roanoke Island? They should not have gone. They went with White, and never made it.

May 6. On the open sea, a French pirate ship spotted the *Brave* and gave chase. Tall-masted, one hundred tons, it bristled with cannon, carrying eighty-four men armed with muskets and pistols. The *Brave*, loaded down with supplies, could not outrun it. "It was in vain to seek flight," White said, and they had no choice but to "fight to help ourselves." The French ship latched on to the *Brave* and pirates spilled aboard, grappling hand to hand with the English sailors "without ceasing, one hour and a half."

Belowdecks, pirates broke into White's supplies, hacking into kegs of flour and meat, destroying everything that might have saved the colonists. Thinking of Eleanor, White lunged to save them. A sword glinted through the air and struck him in

The Spanish Armada was the largest and most frightening navy in the world.

the head. A whirring pike followed. Staggering away, he was shot. Three of the male colonists were also severely hurt. How many survived? Maybe some, maybe none. The *Brave* surrendered and limped back to England, its captain dead, its supplies all gone.

While White recovered — one imagines him hobbling about on crutches — England's day of reckoning was at hand. On the morning of July 19, 1588, Spain's Invincible Armada rose up out of the sea: 20,000 soldiers, 8,350 sailors, 2,630 cannon, 130 warships with their bows carved into angry lions, tigers, and dragons. The massive galleons fanned out in a frightening arc, appearing "with lofty turrets like castles, in front like a half-moon, the wings spreading out about the length of seven miles, sailing very slowly." Nothing like it had ever been seen before.

Yet if the Spanish had hoped to terrify England into submission, they had not counted on Raleigh. Realizing England's ships were no match against Spain's enormous men-of-war, he had urged the queen to redesign her navy. She did, according to Raleigh's plans, streamlining her ships until they could turn with agility around the ponderous Spanish galleons. The Lord Admiral commanded Raleigh's own vessel in the fray, his sleek ship thundering "thick and furiously." The English navy had

THE ARK ROYAL, THE FLAG-SHIP OF THE ENGLISH FLEET.

Raleigh's own ship, the Ark Royal, *led the navy against the Spanish Armada.*

become a marvel, charging "the enemy with wonderful agility and nimbleness."

Never was a victory so triumphant! England won, when no one had thought it could. Without vast armies, without huge amounts of money, England's small navy crushed the largest sea power in the world. Spain's losses were appalling: Of its ninety-one great galleons, fifty-eight were destroyed or missing, and "of [the] 30,000 persons which went in this expedition, there perished . . . the greater and better part."

Rejoicing exploded across England. Cheering crowds filled the streets, and the whole country lit up with a blaze of bonfires. There were parades and wild celebrations with fireworks and dancing, the festivities exceeding anything in modern memory. Justice had triumphed over evil. The queen's popularity soared to frenzied levels.

England's astounding victory was largely due to Raleigh and the changes he had made to the navy. He had saved the day. Yet strangely, in the weeks following the battle, Raleigh appeared to have fallen out of the queen's good graces. Walsingham, whom Elizabeth ordinarily disliked, was for the first time in his life a favorite. What had happened?

CHAPTER 9
out of favor

At Whitehall Palace, no one stayed popular long. Everyone knew it. Envy knocked down rivals, while opponents jockeyed for position and royal favor. There were far more hopefuls than rewards to go around.

Raleigh's star, once the highest and brightest at court, had already begun to set in the autumn of 1586 when Lane returned from his killing field at Dasamonquepeuc. Immediately after he came back, rumors began to fly that Roanoke was barren and hardly worth visiting. Raleigh's friends knew the foul reports came from jealousy. Jealousy made enemies, and Raleigh was too lucky. He was too rich.

The slander had its effect. Investors in Raleigh's expeditions began to waver. There the story might have ended: Interest in

Roanoke faded; Raleigh's base would not be built. No new voyages would have been made — had it not been for John White's colonists, who stepped forward with their own money to start a colony.

From the start, White spoke of enemies who were against the project. Were any of them "Walsingham's men"? Was Lane? He was in contact with Walsingham by letter from Roanoke in 1585, sending numerous notes to the secretary, which he sent home on Grenville's ship.

The year after Lane's return, when White rushed back to London with his incredible story of sabotage and betrayal, the timing was poor. Spain was about to launch the Armada, and the queen needed Walsingham's spy network. She could afford no mistakes. Raleigh complained about Walsingham, and the queen got angry at Raleigh.

At the same time, Raleigh came under stinging attack from a young nobleman new to court. He was the Earl of Essex, and he was Walsingham's son-in-law. Essex went to work, turning the nobility against Raleigh for being a commoner with no right to be at the palace. Gossip flew. Raleigh was termed arrogant and selfish, while Queen Elizabeth herself came under scathing criticism for having been swayed by him. She had given too much support to his Roanoke venture.

The malice reached its peak during a performance for the

queen, when comedian Richard Tarleton, pointing to Raleigh, cried out that the servant ruled the queen! Raleigh was fast becoming the most hated man in the kingdom. Lies made even his friends mistrust him.

As Elizabeth cooled toward Raleigh, she gave Walsingham greater attention. After the defeat of the Armada in 1588, she made him a duke by granting him the duchy of Lancaster. Raleigh, who had redesigned

In 1588, the queen needed Walsingham's spy network.

the navy's ships, got nothing. Indeed, while England was celebrating its victory over Spain, he was sent away from court to clear the coast of Spanish wrecks. Certainly there were deputies who could have done the job so that Raleigh could have enjoyed the festivities. The talk of the town was that he had taken too much credit for the defeat of the Armada. It was better to send him away.

Raleigh returned to Whitehall Palace only to have Essex

challenge him to a duel. When Raleigh refused, Essex's friends had a field day. Raleigh was a troublemaker, they said. He had upset Essex. He disturbed the peace.

With little reason to stay at court, Raleigh left "the passion of his enemies" and retreated to Ireland, only to be trailed by new rounds of slander. London tongues wagged that he had been driven from town, while even his friends — including John White perhaps? — came under attack until they were made to seem "both strange and wild."

In Ireland, Raleigh poured out his bitterness with his pen, scrawling masses of poetry about betrayal. His "Oceans to Cynthia," a letter in verse to the queen, is considered to be one of the best poems in Elizabethan literature.

> *Yet more than this, a hope still found in vain,*
> *A vile despair, that speaks but of distress;*
> *A forc'd content, to suffer deadly pain,*
> *A pain so great, as cannot get redress;*
> *Will all affirm, my sum of sorrow such,*
> *As never man, that ever knew so much.*

Was Raleigh thinking of White's colonists when he wrote these lines? "Vile despair," "distress," and "deadly pain without redress" surely described his frame of mind, and

White's; both of them "knew so much" — too much — about Walsingham. To make his point clearer, Raleigh wrote a ballad about deception, and set it to a tune, called "Walsingham."

In his verses to Queen Elizabeth, Raleigh admitted to having written something to her in "furious madness" that had only made her angry. When he'd told her of a "secret murder done of late," she had only blamed him for mistrusting other people. He accused someone, and the queen refused to believe it. Slander had already labeled John White a liar. "If I complain," Raleigh wrote, "my witness is suspect." White, like Rastell seventy years before, would take the fall for the Lost Colony sabotage.

Meanwhile, White remained in England, scouring the wharves for a way back to Roanoke. Did the Lost Colonists think they had been forgotten? More than a year had passed since he left them forlorn on the beach and promised them a swift return. They would never know how he had tried to save them, pleading with anyone who would listen.

The next year, 1589, Raleigh renewed his effort to reach Roanoke. He no longer had the money to finance another trip, having spent it on the previous rescue fleet. Without the queen's help, he could only ask wealthy investors to send out a an expedition. But they weren't interested. Another year passed.

February 1590 found White in London, and very excited. Three ships were anchored in the Thames, headed for the Caribbean. Would they take him to Roanoke? Before he could find out, the Privy Council dashed his hopes by again confining all ships to port. White was stunned. Then shock gave way to hope, for all three captains were clearly planning to ignore the order. Leaving London, they sailed down to Plymouth harbor, White reported to Raleigh, "absolutely determined to go for the West Indies." As Lord Lieutenant of Cornwall and Devon, with policing duties along the coast, Raleigh had a duty to stop them. Instead, White urged Raleigh to make a deal: let the ships leave if they would agree to take him to Roanoke.

Raleigh was quick to act. With permission from the queen, he wrote a letter to John Watts, the ships' owner, offering to release his vessels in return for transporting White, colonists, and supplies to Roanoke. White waited anxiously for his reply. What would it be?

Watts was known to everyone in London. Freewheeling capitalist and head of the city's great business syndicates, Watts was a flashy man who went around town in costly clothes, with jewels and chains of gold. Watts was rich from shipping. Watts was also a pirate. Spain, which had good reason to know, said that of all the pirates on the high seas, Watts was the most notorious. In fact, his three ships, the *Hopewell*, the *Little John*, and their supply ship the *John Evangelist*, were headed to the West Indies for only one reason: to plunder Spanish posts and attack the treasure fleet. It was hardly the kind of ride White could have desired.

A letter arrived from Watts, accepting Raleigh's deal. White rushed to Plymouth while his colonists hastily packed. Yet when he reached the ships, he was dealt another crippling blow. Captain Abraham Cocke of the *Hopewell* and Captain Christopher Newport of the *Little John* greeted him coldly, refusing to take either colonists or supplies on board. White's

Typical London merchant in the 16th century.

old friend Captain Spicer, who had brought him home from Roanoke, commanded the *John Evangelist*. Surprisingly, even he showed no compassion; or maybe he couldn't. Empty holds meant more plunder could be taken. Spicer worked for Watts. White was allowed a single chest and nothing more.

In agony, White pleaded with the captains and with Watts, sending "daily and continual petitions" to them, begging them to change their minds. It did no good. Watts had broken his promise, and White received only "cross and unkind dealing." Raleigh was far away in London. There was no time left to reach him.

What choice did White have? Three years had passed — three years wasted — and still he could not help the colonists. For this, he had been harassed, slandered, wounded, and shot. If he boarded the *Hopewell* without supplies, he would not be helping them. If he boarded the *Hopewell* without supplies, he could do no more than share the colonists' fate.

March 20, 1590: John White stepped aboard the *Hopewell*. There was no turning back.

CHAPTER 10
An Island Lies Empty

As the Hopewell sailed out of Plymouth harbor, White stood on deck as he had stood with his family on the *Lion* so many years ago. His emotions must have been a painful mix of dread and anticipation: happiness to see them again if they were even alive — and disappointment at his own failure. He would arrive without supplies, and the colonists would know they were abandoned forever.

The ill luck that had stood plagued White on other ocean voyages was with him again, for the *Hopewell* was in no hurry to cross the Atlantic. The Spanish treasure fleet would not reach the Caribbean until June. The ships had plenty of time. In the Canary Islands, Captains Cocke and Newport engaged in a skirmish with a merchant ship, a deadly signal for what lay ahead. White was on a ship that cared nothing for his colonists.

At the end of April, the *Hopewell* entered the Caribbean and separated from the *Little John*. Each went its own way, passing silently through the islands, searching. Off Puerto Rico, the *Hopewell* captured its first prey, a Spanish frigate. But what awful fate! One of its sailors escaped to shore and told the island's governor about the *Hopewell* and its passenger, John White. The governor thought the story sounded familiar. He had been told a similar tale about John White and his colonists by Darby Glande three years before. He had assumed then that Glande had lied, for three years of searching for Roanoke had turned up nothing. Now John White himself was aboard the *Hopewell*, bound for the same English settlement.

The governor's reaction is a clue. We now know that Spain had not harmed the Lost Colonists, though it had certainly tried. The Spanish had simply not found them. Roanoke was too well hidden. Darby Glande had failed.

Once again, White was in a race against time. Spain was alerted, and the *Hopewell* must reach Roanoke without wasting any more time. But the treasure fleet had not yet appeared, and Captain Cocke let days slip into weeks, waiting for it. Meanwhile, reports of pirates streamed in to Spanish officials as the *Hopewell* hovered off Cuba, chasing every ship that entered the harbor.

At last, the treasure fleet was spotted off the coast of Jamaica, and the *Hopewell* moved in and attacked. Counting their losses, infuriated Spanish authorities stepped up their efforts to locate Roanoke to put an end to England's colony. Spain had no way of knowing that White's settlement was no threat to anyone. The Lost Colonists had been left for dead.

It was not until August 1 that the *Hopewell* finally turned north, anchoring off Hatorask Island two weeks later. White stood on deck in the gathering dusk, hardly believing that he was back. After so many years of struggle, he had finally returned! White gazed at the distant beach, empty except for a flock of sandpipers scurrying along the sand.

Sandpipers on the beach at Hatorask (today's Nag's Head).

But not empty. A column of smoke suddenly began to rise from the trees in the direction of Roanoke. White could hardly contain his joy. The ships had been seen! The smoke proved that at least "some of the colony were there, expecting my return." Too late to go ashore, White went to bed, much against his will, condemned to a long and sleepless night.

At the first blush of dawn, at White's urging, the *Hopewell's* master gunner fired the cannon, so that the noise would be heard by the colonists. As shots cracked the air, White climbed into a shore boat and was lowered into the sea. The sailors had rowed him halfway to land when suddenly a second billowing smoke was spotted on Hatorask Island in the opposite direction from the first. Were there two groups of people? The second smoke was closer. White went there first.

On Hatorask, after walking miles through sandy scrub, which took over several hours — the fire being much farther away than it looked — White again met with stinging disappointment. The smoke was nothing more than trees burning from a fire that appeared to have been set by lightning in a recent storm. "We found," said White, "no man nor sign that any had been there lately." A whole day had been wasted. The trip to Roanoke would have to wait again.

August 17. White arose as the early morning sun spread its rays across the water. He was eager to reach Roanoke. Yet to his dismay, Spicer's sailors had taken the boat ashore to refill casks of water, and Captain Cocke refused to launch the other boat without them. White stared numbly at Roanoke, its outline visible on the horizon. He was so close, yet so very far.

At ten o'clock, Spicer's crew finally returned. Both shore boats were hurriedly got under way. Yet the morning's delay had been costly. The tide had turned and a gusting wind had risen, churning up the channel between the barrier islands. Dark waves crashed angrily against one another, sending up a foaming spray. White's boat surged forward into the rushing water, "not without some danger of sinking." A swell smashed into the boat, spinning it around, but Captain Cocke managed to wrench it back before the next wave hit. Only "by the will of God," remarked White, had they been saved. The sailors drew the boat onto the beach at Hatorask and poured the water out of it. Food and clothing were lugged out onto the sand to dry. Everything was wet.

The sailors joined White at the water's edge to wait for Spicer, whose boat was then approaching the channel. But Spicer had made a fatal mistake: He had forgotten to lower the mast. The watchers scarcely dared breathe as the boat entered the boiling channel, tipping crazily into the waves as the mast threw it off balance. The master's mate struggled to right it, but he lost control and the hull swung broadside into a wave. The next instant, "a very dangerous sea broke into their boat and overset them." White watched in horror as the boat went over, its crew clinging helplessly to its side as a swell rammed it hard onto a sandbar. The sailors staggered to their feet and tried to wade toward land, but the sea "beat them down, so that they could neither stand nor swim." Three times the boat's keel rose high into the air, towering over them, while Captain Spicer and his mate dangled from it, struggling to hang on. Then the boat pitched sideways, and both men were drowned.

Captain Cocke dove into the water to rescue the sailors, but most of them, who had spent their entire lives at sea, had never learned to swim. Of eleven of Spicer's men, only four survived. Among the drowned was a surgeon, who was not able to save himself, let alone the colonists he had come to see.

The accident terrorized the sailors. Every one of them refused to go farther. White frantically pleaded with them, begging, demanding. They must take him to Roanoke! It had been three long years since he had gone away! His daughter, his granddaughter were there. He must reach them! Roanoke — he pointed — was within view. The channel had been crossed; they must go forward!

The sailors stared at him wildly, with fear in their eyes. It wasn't until half a day had passed and the waves had calmed that Spicer's boat was finally dragged out of the water and the men persuaded to get back into it. They set off for Roanoke as the sun began to fade.

Night crept over the island long before John White reached it. Roanoke loomed out of the water, blacker than the surrounding blackness, full of the smell of earth and loblolly. White directed the boats to the part of the island where he had left his colonists, but in the darkness they overshot the spot. Hugging the shoreline, they had no sooner turned back when a light suddenly appeared in the woods, flickering dimly through the trees. White ordered the men to stop, and as they peered closer, they saw that the light was actually a fire crackling some distance from the shore. One of the sailors grabbed a trumpet and sounded a call, then waited, hoping for an answer. Silence fell around the boat. White leaped up and urged the men to shout! To sing! To make noise! And they did, chanting "many familiar English tunes of songs." And still no sound came back to them but the lapping of waves. White then yelled, and the sailors joined him, mingling their cries with words of greeting, calling the colonists' names — names that had not been spoken in three long years. Their voices trailed off into silence. "We had no answer," White said miserably.

The next morning, day three of his awful vigil, White hurried ashore. Rushing through the woods toward the previous night's fire, he burst in upon a clearing filled with smoldering wood, but nothing else. No one was there. Someone must have lit the fire, but they were gone. There was no camp of any kind.

Afraid now for the fate of his family, White raced back along the shore, toward the place of the settlement. The sailors followed as best they could, not knowing what to expect, or what to look for. On the beach, they stumbled across footprints left in the sand, made by more than one person during the night. While the sailors had sung and White had shouted, someone had been there in the darkness, listening.

Farther down the beach, White made another startling discovery. On the bark of a tree growing out of the sandy bank were carved these three letters: CRO.

White studied the word, but did not know what it meant, nor did the sailors. CRO spelled nothing! No word, no name. If it was intended as a message, it failed, for no amount of discussion could make any sense of it. Quickly making his way to the fort where he had left the colonists, White stopped short, dumbfounded. The sailors behind him also stopped and stared, for there was nothing before them but an empty clearing. Did White have the right location? How could he? Gone were the houses, the casks, the kettles. Gone were the fort ruins, the chests and tools. Nothing was left, not even the people. No one remained.

Surrounding the area where the houses had been was a

*The letters "CRO" meant little to White since other Secotan towns began with
these letters. "Croatoan" meant "talk town," a place where councils were held.*

wooden stockade. White moved closer to examine it, for nothing like it had been there before, and he suddenly noticed that
carved on it was the word: Croatoan. White's frown turned to
laughter and he whooped aloud, for he knew that place.
Croatoan was the island "where Manteo was born," and the
people were "our friends."

The colonists had done as White had directed. They had left him the name of the place they had gone. But what of his other instructions? If the colonists were in danger, he had told them to carve a cross above the name, like this: +. White ran trembling fingers over the letters etched into the post. The colonists had not been in danger. There was no cross!

In his mind's eye, White must have imagined the colonists' final days on Roanoke Island. As they stood on shore, watching his boat disappear on the horizon, had they given in to despair? Had they panicked? By the look of it, they had done neither, but had filled their days with action. Someone — Ananias, perhaps? — had directed the men to build the stockade for their own protection. White was amazed at its construction, for it had "curtains and flankers, very fort-like." With such a wall, they could guard against Spanish or Secotan attack, while they dismantled the houses.

But no attack ever came. Darby Glande did not know where Roanoke was, and Spanish parties never found it. Where the Spaniards failed, White succeeded, for his message of peace had reached the Secotan. Wanchese and the survivors at Dasamonquepeuc had not come forward in friendship, but they had not come as enemies either. There was no cross. They had left the colonists alone. This is a clue to understanding them, too. They were unwilling — despite all their suffering — to punish the innocent for what Lane had done. Their treatment of White's colonists showed true kindness of heart.

Inside the palisade, the Lost Colonists' meager goods had been packed. The houses were taken down and loaded aboard a small boat they had. Walking to a nearby creek, White and Captain Cocke discovered the little boat missing. Of the vessel itself, we do not know much: only that it was too small to cross the Atlantic, or White would have assumed they attempted it. In his letters, he made it clear that he never thought they had. The boat was able to carry boards and chests through the sound and up the rivers for one trip . . . several trips. The only things the colonists had left behind were heavy iron goods and the fort's old cannon, too weighty to be floated. In the sand, the sailors discovered five large chests, three of them White's, that had been buried and long since dug up, perhaps by the Secotan. The colonists had left in an orderly fashion. Their departure was unhurried, perhaps even calm. There was no cross. There were no dead bodies, no new graves. When the colonists left Roanoke, they were still all right.

The information that his family was safe at Croatoan must have come to White as a welcome surprise. At the time of his departure, they had talked about moving "fifty miles farther up into the main" — the mainland of the continent toward the

Chowanoc country, not south along the coast to Croatoan. Still, White must have been pleased. The colonists were nearby, and with much eagerness he left the clearing that contained so many memories, and led the sailors back to the boats. They made their way to the Hopewell, he said, "with as much speed as we could."

The trip was difficult. Another strong wind had blown in, turning the water into a rough chop. The sailors, mindful of the seven men swallowed by the sea only the day before, were tense. They pulled hard at the oars, their muscles straining against the waves and the wind, and made little headway. It was not until evening, and after "much danger and labour," that they finally reached the Hopewell. The peak hurricane season had arrived.

That night, while the crew wondered if the anchors would hold against the wind, White confronted Captain Cocke and begged him to set a course for Croatoan. Outside, an anchor spun away. Then another. Then another. Shouting above the storm, the captain at last agreed. He would stop at Croatoan, then return home.

But the storm worsened. With only one anchor left and the ship veering toward the shoals, Captain Cocke fiercely cut the ship loose and ran it into deeper water. The rough seas continued until August 28. Then the wind shifted, and the hurricane hit. It

*As White discovered, violent storms rush onto the
Secotan coast during hurricane season.*

came exploding up from Croatoan, pounding the ship with howling winds and monstrous seas as lightning bolts rained down. Helpless before the gale, the *Hopewell* was driven east across the Atlantic, far from the Secotan country. White was desperate. He must have been, for he pleaded with Captain Cocke again and again, as the storm subsided, to return to Croatoan, urging him to spend the winter in the Caribbean where he could take more Spanish plunder if he liked. White almost convinced him.

Reaching the Azores, halfway across the ocean, the *Hopewell* encountered the *Little John*, last seen battling Spanish ships in the Caribbean. Its captain, Christopher Newport, had been hurt: His arm had been struck off with a sword. The *Hopewell*'s sailors saw this and grew disheartened. There was no point in returning to the Caribbean; the treasure fleet had already passed that year and the Spaniards were obviously very much on their guard. Captain Cocke made his decision. White watched, stunned, as he set a course for England.

On October 24, it was over. The *Hopewell* came to anchor in Plymouth harbor. Three years later, writing from Ireland, White was finally able to talk about his loss in a note to a friend:

"Thus you may plainly perceive the success of my fifth and last voyage," he wrote, "which was no less unfortunately ended than begun, and as luckless to many as sinister to myself. . . . Yet seeing it is not my first crossed voyage, I remain contented, . . . committing the relief of my discomfortable company, the planters, to the merciful help of the Almighty, whom I most humbly beseech to help and comfort them, according to his most Holy will and their good desire. . . . Your most well wishing friend, John White."

After this letter, John White was never heard from again.

CHAPTER 11
Epilogue

When John White returned to England in October 1590, he certainly met with Raleigh about the Lost Colonists. Had either man been able to afford it, a rescue expedition would have left for Croatoan at once. Meanwhile, Raleigh's troubles at court continued. A booklet was published blaming him for the deaths of voyagers and sailors. Was this referring to the Lost Colonists and Spicer's crew? Yet it wasn't Raleigh who had caused their plight, and perhaps the Lost Colonists were still alive.

Then another rumor surfaced: Raleigh was secretly married to Elizabeth Throckmorton, one of the queen's maids of honor! Some said they had married years before, at about the time White reported the Roanoke sabotage. If the queen had got wind of it then, no wonder her anger at Raleigh had been so great! In July 1592, the truth came out — and for once the rumors were right. Raleigh and Elizabeth Throckmorton had married. In a rage, Queen Elizabeth hurled the lovers into the Tower. Tourists who came to watch the lions and tigers now strained for a glimpse of Raleigh.

In October, the queen released both Raleigh and his wife from prison, but banished them from court for five years. Did Raleigh think of the Lost Colonists during any of this time? He evidently did. Information that Raleigh may have tried to rescue them in 1594 was reported to Spain, strange as it sounds, by none other than Darby Glande. Glande was then in Cuba and

The Tower of London, a fortress palace belonging to the queen, was long used as a prison and a zoo, caging men and animals. Raleigh spent thirteen years imprisoned here.

had heard the story from English sailors. Raleigh, they said, had sent two rescue ships to Roanoke. If true, they hadn't found the colonists, as later events would prove. Then again, neither had Spain. Others in 1594 were not so optimistic about their survival. The Lost Colonists

Raleigh's cell in the Tower of London was two small rooms, one atop the other.

had been missing for seven years, and English law pronounced them dead.

In 1597, the sixty-four-year-old queen welcomed Raleigh back to court, and he immediately renewed his search for White's family. By 1602, he had made five rescue attempts. Each failed to reach Croatoan, but Raleigh kept trying.

In March 1602, he bought his own ship. Paying the sailors in order to keep them from plundering Spanish ships, Raleigh sent them to Roanoke with instructions to "find those people which were left there in the year 1587." Samuel Mace led the expedition. Scientist Thomas Hariot carefully coached him before he left, teaching him Secotan words.

Mace failed like all the rest. He landed on the coast far south of the Secotan country, and storms drove him back before he could reach Croatoan. The next spring, in May 1603, Raleigh tried again. This time, he sent a search party to the Chesapeake Bay to see if the colonists had gone there. The crew found

Long, mournful processions accompanied Queen Elizabeth's
body to Westminster Abbey, where she was buried.

nothing. They returned to London, only to find everything changed. Raleigh had been arrested.

In 1618, King James I had Raleigh beheaded as part of a peace agreement James made with Spain.

London, 1603. In March, London was rocked by news of Queen Elizabeth's death. The seventy-year-old monarch was at Richmond Palace when she died, a residence she considered more comfortable than Whitehall. She had been complaining of a swollen throat and difficulty swallowing.

While the kingdom mourned, the queen's courtiers scrambled to convince England's new monarch, King James of Scotland, of their loyalty. The king arrived in London in May, the same month that Raleigh sent his search party to the Chesapeake Bay.

In the months before the queen died, Raleigh's enemies had been in touch with King James, warning him that Raleigh could not be trusted. With Elizabeth dead, Raleigh had no protector. His friendship with her fanned the king's distrust.

On November 17, 1603, without a shred of evidence or a

Young Prince Henry, King James I's son, adored Raleigh and tried, unsuccessfully, to obtain his release from the Tower.

lawyer to defend him, with a jury made up of his enemies appointed by the King, Raleigh was tried, convicted, and sentenced to death on the charge of treason. It was later discovered that four of the seven-man jury had received payments from Spain.

"Thou art a monster!" the king's attorney-general shouted at Raleigh during the trial. A "viper!" A snake.

Raleigh had spent a lifetime fighting Spain. He had led Elizabeth's navy to victory against them at Cadiz. He had founded an English colony in America, a territory that Spain itself had claimed. It was Raleigh's redesigned ships that had defeated the Armada, the greatest navy that had ever put to sea. There was no man in England that Spain hated more.

After the trial, English public opinion surged in favor of Raleigh. Sailors, workers, and rural people called for justice while mobs formed in the West Country where he was born. Under pressure, James backed down. Raleigh was not put to death, but condemned to life imprisonment in the Tower, banished — like the Lost Colonists — from the world.

In the four hundred years since the disappearance of White's settlement, it has been said repeatedly that the Lost Colonists were never seen again. In fact, the colonists *were* seen, more than once.

Twenty years after their disappearance, strange stories began to surface at the newly settled Jamestown colony, of Englishmen held captive deep in the interior. The Powhatan were insistent on this point. They repeatedly told Captain John Smith of white people wearing English clothes who lived in two-story houses. Smith rushed search teams to the places indicated only to learn that the Mandoag had captured them all. Survivors were taken to the great Occaneechi trade mart and whisked away to interior nations. Some were kept as slaves to work the copper mines of Chaunis Temoatan. The investigators were not allowed to speak to any of them, though they were there in a forest of trees etched with crosses. Small and weak, Jamestown hadn't the power to bring them home. So they told a lie: The colonists, they said, were all dead. And thus the search ended.

There was one clue about the Lost Colonists that was uncovered at Croatoan and not deep in the interior. In 1701, fully 114 years after the disappearance of the Lost Colony, surveyor John Lawson visited the island. He had begun his trek from newly settled Charleston, South Carolina, and had traveled north to the Outer Banks in the Secotan country. On Hatorask Island, as he busily took measurements of the coast, a group of Secotan gathered around. They were familiar with English traders and were able to converse with Lawson. They told him that they lived on Roanoke Island, or visited there often. Watching him jot down notes, they then startled him with the remark that "several of their ancestors were white people, and could talk in a book as we do." Astonished, Lawson peered at them closely, and was stunned. The truth of their claim, he admitted, was "confirmed by grey eyes being found frequently amongst these Indians." Could this mean that at least some of the Lost Colonists went to Croatoan as White supposed, and lived with the Secotan, intermarrying with them? Lawson thought so. On foggy days, the Secotan told him, they often saw the ship that brought White's colonists to Roanoke, appearing off the coast under full sail, "which they call Sir Walter Raleigh's ship."

Ghost ships. The rescue parties sent out by Raleigh had become the stuff of legend.

Roanoke Time Line

1584 EXPEDITION 1 ~ led by Captains Philip Amadas and
Arthur Barlowe. Purpose: to explore the Secotan country,
to find a base to use against the Spanish treasure fleet.

1585 EXPEDITION 2 ~ led by Sir Richard Grenville.
Purpose: military, to build a fort from which to attack Spain.
Captain Ralph Lane spends the winter at the fort, attacking the
Secotan and Chowanoc instead.

1586 June. Sir Francis Drake visits the Secotan country and
carries Lane and his soldiers back to England.

1586 EXPEDITION 3 ~ led by Grenville.
Purpose: to bring supplies to Lane's soldiers.
Grenville leaves fifteen men to occupy the deserted fort.

1587 EXPEDITION 4 ~ led by John White.
Destination: The Chesapeake Bay.
Purpose: to establish the first English colony in America.
White's colonists are marooned on Roanoke Island.

1587 November. White meets with Raleigh in London and
tells him about the sabotage.

1588 March. Raleigh's rescue ships are seized by the Privy Council.

1588 April. John White sails for Roanoke in the *Brave*.
Attacked by pirates, he returns to England wounded.

1588 July. England is victorious over the Spanish Armada.
Raleigh withdraws to Ireland. White tries to find a way back to Roanoke.

1589 March. Raleigh forms a group of investors to send
rescue ships to Roanoke Island. He is unable to raise the money.

1590 March. White sails to Roanoke on the *Hopewell*, a pirate ship
owned by John Watts. White reaches Roanoke to find the colonists gone.

1597~1602 Raleigh sends out five different missions to rescue
the Lost Colonists. None succeed.

1603 March. Queen Elizabeth dies at the age of 70.

1603 May. King James arrives in London.

1603 July. Raleigh is falsely charged with treason and thrown
into the Tower.

1607 Jamestown is settled. Clues are discovered.

1608~1610 Search teams are sent from Jamestown to hunt for
the Lost Colonists. They report numerous clues and a sighting.

source notes

Note: Ibid. is short for the Latin word Ibidem *that means "in the same place." The notation means the quote comes from the same source as the one above it.*

Op. cit. is an abbreviation of the Latin words opera citato *that mean "in the work cited." Op. cit. is used when the book has already been listed. It is followed by the author's last name and a few words of the title. Look above to find the book the quote comes from.*

Pages 9, 17, 18: Barlowe, Arthur, " The first voyage made to the coastes of America" (1589) in Hakluyt, Richard, *Principall Navigations, Voiages, Traffiques and Discoveries of the English Nation*, first edition, 1589, second edition, 1598 – 1600, 3 vols: includes Barlowe.

Page 21: "good sailors . . ." Hentzner, Paul, *Travels in England*, 1598, reprinted by William Rye, *England as Seen by Foreigners*, London: J. R. Smith, 1865, p. 110.

Page 21: names of ship: Andrews, Kenneth, *Elizabethan Privateering: English Privateering during the Spanish War, 1585 – 1603*, Cambridge: Cambridge University Press, 1964, pp. 289 – 294.

Pages 27, 29, 31, 32: Hariot, Thomas, "A Briefe and True Report of the New Found Land of Virginia, 1588" printed in Hakluyt, *Principall Navigations*, cited above.

Page 39: food statistics: Williams, Neville, *Elizabeth: Queen of England*, London: Weidenfeld & Nicolson, 1967, pp. 221 – 4.

Page 41: ". . . it were a dog . . ." Harrison, William, *The Description of England*, 1587, London: J. Johnson, et al., 1807, vol. 1, p. 289.

Page 41: "monstrous" Stubbes, Philip, *The Anatomie of Abuses*, 1583, p. Eii.

Page 41: London saying: Camden, William, *Remains Concerning Britain*, 1674, orig. 1586, p. 327.

Page 46: White, John. "The fourth voyage made to Virginia" (1589) printed in Hakluyt, *Principall Navigations*, cited above.

Page 50: "to a great joy . . ." Ibid.

Page 51 – 52: Ibid.

Page 67: " a diligent searcher . . ." Camden, William, *The History of the Most Renowned and Victorious Princess Elizabeth, Late Queen of England*, 1688, orig. 1615, p. 444.

Page 68: "Walsingham's man" Anonymous, *Brief Description of the People*, 1607, PRO State Papers Colonial, Great Britain, Public Record Office, C.O. 1/1, 2.

Page 69: " In court, camp . . ." Shirley, John, *The Life of the Valiant and Learned Sir Walter Raleigh, Knight. With His Trial at Winchester*, 1677, p. 242.

Page 69: "He was no slug." Aubrey, John. *Brief Lives*, printed from Bodleian and Ashmolean mss, ed. Andrew Clark. Oxford: Clarendon Press, 1898, vol. II, p. 190.

Page 70: "could overthrow . . ." Lloyd, David, *State-Worthies; or, the Statesmen and Favourites of England*, 1670, p. 515.

Page 71: "strange and wonderful . . ." Van Meteren, Emanuel, "The Miraculous Victory Achieved by the English Fleete," printed and translated by Hakluyt, *Principall Navigations*, cited above.

Page 72: "yet by order . . ." Rowse, A.L. *Sir Richard Grenville of the Revenge*. London: Jonathan Cape, 1949, p. 264.

Page 73, all: op.cit., Hakluyt, *Principall Navigations*, pp. 771 – 773.

Page 75: " with lofty turrets . . ." op.cit., Camden, *The History of the Most Renowned . . .*, p. 404.

Page 75: "thick and furiously." Ibid, p. 411.

Page 80: "the passion of his enemies" Naunton, Robert, *Fragmenta Regalia; or, observations on Queen Elizabeth, Her Times & Favourites*, 2nd edition, 1641, reprinted in *The Harleian Miscellany*, v, London: for Robert Dutton, 1810, p. 145.

Page 80: "both strange and wild." Raleigh, Walter. "Ocean to Scinthia," Hatfield ms, Cecil Papers, 144. Hatfield House. 11th book, lines 267–8.

Page 80: "Oceans to Cynthia." Latham, Agnes M. C., ed., *The Poems of Sir Walter Raleigh*. Cambridge, Mass.: Harvard University Press, 1959. pp 22 – 3.

Page 81: "furious madness" op.cit., Raleigh, "Ocean to Scinthia," 11th book, line 145.

Page 81: "secret murder done of late." Raleigh, Walter. *The Phoenix Nest, R.S.*, ed. 1593.

Page 81: "If I complain . . ." Raleigh, Walter. "Wounded I am . . ." in William Byrd (ed.), *Songs of Sundrie Natures*, 1589.

Page 82: "absolutely determined" op.cit., Hakluyt, *Principall Navigations*, vol. III.

Page 83: " daily and continual petitions" Ibid.

Pages 88 – 98: all John White quotes Ibid.

Page 101: "find those people . . ." Brereton, John, *A Briefe and True Relation of the Discoverie of the North Part of Virginia*, 1602. p 14.

Page 103 – 4: "Thou art a monster . . ." Hawks, Francis L., *History of North Carolina*, Fayetteville, N. C.: E. J. Hale, 1857. vol 1, pp 47 – 49.

INDEX

*Numbers in **bold** denote illustration*

PHOTO CREDITS: Pages 1, 6, 14, 15, 17, 28, 44–45, 87: Lee Miller; Page 9: Thomas Mangelsen/Minden Pictures; Pages 2, 10, 12, 13, 16, 20 (bottom), 21, 24, 25, 26, 29, 30, 33, 36–37, 39, 40, 41, 53, 57, 58, 63, 64, 67, 74, 79, 83, 93, 103, 104: The Granger Collection, New York; Page 20 (top): Portrait of Queen Elizabeth I (1533–1603) in Ceremonial Costume (oil on canvas), Zuccari, or Zuccaro, Federico (1540–1609)/Pinacoteca Nazionale, Siena, Italy, Alinari/The Bridgeman Art Library; Page 27: Charles Nicholl, *The Reckoning: The Murder of Christopher Marlowe*, Chicago: University of Chicago Press, 1995, Plate 9; Page 38: Art Resource, NY; Page 45: George H. H. Huey/Corbis; Page 46: Fortified Encampment, Puerto Rico (litho), White, John (fl. 1570–93) (after)/Private Collection/The Bridgeman Art Library; Page 62: Robert Dudley, Earl of Leicester (c. 1532–88) c. 1565–70 (oil on panel), English School (16th century)/© National Gallery of Victoria, Melbourne, Australia, Felton Bequest/The Bridgeman Art Library; Page 65: Lord Burghley (1520–98), English School (16th century)/Burghley House Collection, Lincolnshire, UK/The Bridgeman Art Library; Page 66: Western Façade (photo) (see also 58475)/Burghley House, Stamford, Lincolnshire, UK, Mark Fiennes/The Bridgeman Art Library; Page 67: Tim Hawkins; Eye Ubiquitous/Corbis; Pages 75, 102: Bettmann/Corbis; Page 97: Ray Matthews; Pages 100, 101: Angelo Hornak/Corbis.

Library of Congress Cataloging-in-Publication Data
Miller, Lee • Roanoke: the Mystery of the Lost Colony / by Lee Miller. • p. cm. • ISBN 13: 978-0-439-71266-8 (alk. paper)
ISBN 10: 0-439-71266-1 • 1. Roanoke Colony — Juvenile literature. 2. Roanoke Island (N.C.) — History — 16th century — Juvenile literature. I. Title. • F229.M649 2007 • 975.6'175 — dc22 • 2005051820

10 9 8 7 6 5 4 3 2 1   07 08 09 10 11

Printed in Singapore 46
First printing, April 2007

Text set in 15-point Fournier. Heads set in Americratika.
Book design by Nancy Sabato